This book
belongs to

Walt Disney's

Snow White
AND THE Seven Dwarfs

Adapted by Lisa Ann Marsoli

MOUSE
WORKS

Long, long ago in a magnificent castle, there lived a pretty young princess named Snow White. Her stepmother, the queen, was a wicked woman whose greatest fear was that Snow White's beauty would one day become greater than her own.

And so Snow White was dressed in rags and forced to be her stepmother's servant. Her long days were spent scrubbing floors and cooking meals.

Still, the evil stepmother worried that as Snow White grew, so would her beauty. Every day the queen looked in her magic mirror, anxiously asking: "Magic mirror on the wall, Who is the fairest one of all?"

You are the fairest one of all, the mirror would always reply. And the queen would be content for another day.

Snow White was an obedient stepdaughter who happily did her work while daydreaming of a handsome prince who might one day fall in love with her and take her to live with him in his castle.

One morning, as she drew water from the well, she made a wish that someday her dream would come true.

As if by magic, a handsome young prince
appeared before her. He had been watching Snow
White as she drew water from the well, and was
entranced by her beauty. But Snow White was shy
and fled to the tower balcony. As the prince sang
her a love song below, Snow White placed a kiss
on her friend the dove, who carried it to her beloved.

On that day, the queen's magic mirror told the queen that Snow White was the fairest in all the land. In a jealous rage, the queen called one of her royal huntsmen.

"Take Snow White far into the forest and kill her," she commanded, "and as proof of your deed, bring me back her heart in this." And she handed him a carved box.

The huntsman began his
deadly mission. Telling her
they were going for a walk,
he took Snow White deep
into the forest. Snow White
sang a happy tune, gathering
flowers and thinking of her
handsome prince.

Among the flowers she heard the cry of a baby
bird that had fallen out of its nest. When she found the
little creature, she picked it up and comforted it. "Don't
worry, your mama and papa can't be far," she cooed.
Feeling better, the little bird set off to find its parents.

When they reached the heart of the forest, the huntsman drew his dagger. As he crept up behind Snow White, she turned and screamed, realizing what was about to happen. When the huntsman saw the fear in the princess's eyes, he fell to his knees.

"I beg of you, Your Highness, forgive me," he pleaded. He told Snow White of the queen's jealousy, and how he was ordered to bring Snow White's heart back to the castle as proof of his deed. "Now quick, child," he told her, "Run away! Hide!"

Snow White was very frightened. She gasped, whirled around, and ran into the forest.

The woods were dark and full of strange noises
and frightening sights. As Snow White ran past,
owls hooted and bats beat their wings overhead.
Even the trees seemed to reach out to her with their
branches and watch her with glowing eyes.

Snow White ran faster and faster, and when she could run no more, she fell to the ground and began to weep.

When she had finished crying, Snow White
looked up and found herself surrounded by forest
animals. Slowly they moved closer, realizing that they
had nothing to fear from the kind princess.

The forest creatures comforted their new friend, and soon Snow White was feeling much better. "I do need a place to sleep at night," she told them. "Maybe you know where I can stay. Will you take me there?"

Instantly, two raccoons tugged at the hem of her skirt and began to guide her through the woods. The deer, rabbits, chipmunks, squirrels, and birds followed close behind.

Soon they were at the edge of a clearing. Snow White pushed aside the bushes and saw a charming little cottage nestled among the trees. She ran toward the house, crossing over the little bridge just in front of it, and peered in one of the windows. "I guess there's no one home!" she exclaimed.

Inside the cottage Snow White saw seven little chairs.

"Why, seven little children must live here—seven very untidy children!" she remarked to the animals.

Indeed, wherever Snow White looked she saw dirty dishes, dust on the furniture, and cobwebs everywhere.

"I know, we'll clean the house and surprise them," she told the forest creatures. "Maybe when they see what we've done, they'll let me stay."

Together Snow White and the animals cleaned the little cottage and made it tidy.

When they finished
cleaning downstairs, Snow
White and her friends went
to see what they might find
upstairs. At the top of the
staircase was a door, and
beyond it Snow White saw
seven little beds.

"Look! Each bed has a
name carved on it," Snow
White said, and she read
the names out loud. "Doc,
Happy, Sneezy, Dopey,
Grumpy, Bashful, and
Sleepy."

Snow White yawned. "I'm
a little sleepy myself," she
said. Then she stretched out
across three beds and fell
fast asleep.

Meanwhile, in a nearby mine, the seven dwarfs
were hard at work digging for diamonds. They—not
seven little children—were the ones who lived in the
cottage Snow White had found.

Each dwarf had his own special job to do. Doc stood at a table and peered at the diamonds through a jeweler's glass. He saved the good diamonds and tossed away the bad ones, which Dopey swept up.

As night fell, the dwarfs headed for home. With
their picks slung over their shoulders, the seven dwarfs
marched in a line. Doc took the lead, with Grumpy,
Happy, Sleepy, Sneezy, Bashful, and Dopey following
behind.

Even though they were very hungry and tired from
their hard day's work, the dwarfs sang a happy song
as they marched along.

When the dwarfs
neared their cottage, Doc
stopped in his tracks.

"Look! The lit's light.
I mean, the light's lit!
Somethin's in there!" he
cried.

Though they were
worried that they might
find a ghost or other
scary creature inside,
all the dwarfs bravely
followed Doc into the
house to investigate.

The dwarfs slowly opened the door and crept
into the cottage, trying not to make a sound.

"Careful, men," Doc whispered. The others tiptoed
up behind him.

"Our window's been washed," said Happy.

"Look—the floor! It's sween bept—I mean, been
swept," noticed Doc.

"There's dirty work afoot!" Grumpy grumbled. He
was always suspicious.

Suddenly, they heard a noise upstairs.

"One of us has got to go down and chase it up
...I mean...go up and chase it down," muttered Doc.
The dwarfs quickly elected Dopey to lead the way.

"Don't be afraid. We're right behind you," they all
whispered.

Quietly and carefully, the dwarfs climbed the stairs
one by one until they reached the bedroom. They
inched into the room, and saw a sheeted figure
stretched across the beds.

Snow White yawned and stretched under the
sheet. It was a frightening sight for the poor dwarfs,
who cowered on the floor.

"A monster!" they gasped.

Doc gathered all his courage and pulled back the sheet.

"Why, it's a girl!" he exclaimed.

Snow White was very surprised to see seven dwarfs peering at her from the foot of the bed. "Why, you're not children," she said, sitting up. "You're men!"

Looking at them, Snow White could easily guess the name that belonged to each dwarf. "And you must be Grumpy," she said with a giggle, folding her arms to imitate him.

Then Snow White introduced herself and told the dwarfs about the wicked queen and how the animals had rescued her from the forest. "Please don't send me away," she pleaded. "If you do, the wicked queen will surely find me."

The dwarfs took pity on Snow White. And when she told them that she would clean and cook for them in return for their kindness, they quickly decided that she should stay—all except Grumpy, who simply said, "Hmph." He wanted nothing to do with a wicked queen—or a tidy princess.

Back at the castle, the
huntsman had delivered the
box back to the queen.
He had fooled the queen by
placing a pig's heart inside
it instead of Snow White's.
Thinking Snow White was
dead, the queen eagerly
asked her magic mirror:
"Magic mirror on the wall,
Who now is the fairest one
of all?"

But the mirror replied:
Over the seven jeweled hills,
beyond the seventh fall,
in the cottage of the seven
dwarfs dwells Snow White,
fairest one of all.

The queen was enraged.
Snow White was still alive!

The queen stormed
down the winding
staircase that led to a
dark dungeon beneath
the castle. There she
went to a hidden room
filled with bottles,
potions, and a book
of magic spells. She
opened the book, and,
finding a spell for a
disguise, mixed a
terrible potion. Then
she drank the brew and
was instantly transformed
into an ugly old hag.

Next the queen found another spell and, following the recipe carefully, filled her cauldron with a bubbling liquid. She took an apple and slowly dipped it into the poisonous potion.

"And now," she cackled, "a special sort of death for one so fair. One bite of this poisoned apple and Snow White will close her eyes forever! Then I shall be the fairest of them all once more!"

Far away from the castle dungeon, Snow White and the dwarfs were about to have dinner.

"You'll just have time to wash," Snow White decided. "Let me see your hands."

One by one, the dwarfs slowly took their hands from behind their backs and showed them to Snow White.

"Worse than I thought," she said. "March straight outside and wash, or you'll not get a bite to eat."

The dwarfs didn't really want to wash, but they were willing to do it to make Snow White happy—except Grumpy.

"Her wiles are beginnin' to work!" he muttered. He stood groaning and grumbling as he watched the others. Well, let them—he was not going to wash!

Six dwarfs quickly
scrubbed up. Then they
all turned to Grumpy. And,
before he knew what was
happening, they jumped
on him!

"Get 'im!" shouted Doc.

They grabbed Grumpy
and pulled him over to the
tub, where they washed
his hands and face—even
his beard!

Now all seven were
ready for dinner.

When they had finished
eating, it was time for some fun.
the dwarfs played their musical
instruments while Snow White
danced around the room.

Each dwarf took a
turn dancing with Snow
White. The last was Dopey,
who climbed onto Sneezy's
shoulders and covered
them both up with a long
cloak. Now he was as tall
as Snow White!

But only until Sneezy
sneezed—and sneezed
Dopey right off his
shoulders!

While laughter rang out from the dwarfs' cottage,
the wicked queen began her journey to find Snow
White. Disguised as a peddler woman, she took a boat
across the moat that separated the castle from the
forest. She placed the basket of shiny red apples at her
feet. On top was the poisoned fruit intended for Snow
White.

The next morning, the dwarfs prepared for another day at their diamond mine. Each one said good-bye to Snow White and, as he did, received a kiss on the head in return.

Even Grumpy didn't seem to mind much being kissed by the princess. "Now, I'm warnin' you," he said, "don't let anybody into the house!"

"Why, Grumpy!" she exclaimed. "You do care!"

After she had waved good-bye to the
dwarfs, Snow White decided to make them a pie
for dessert that night. Her animal friends looked
on as she mixed the dough and rolled it out.
She especially wanted to make the pie for
Grumpy, because he seemed to have a sweet
side to him, after all.

While Snow White worked, she thought about
the handsome prince she had met at the castle
well. She wished he would find her—then she
would feel truly safe.

Suddenly the queen, disguised as an old woman, appeared outside the window, interrupting Snow White's daydream. The animals, becoming frightened, scurried away to hide inside cupboards and behind furniture.

"I see you're making a pie," the hag said in a gravelly voice. "And I have just the thing. It's apple pies that make the menfolk's mouths water." She held a beautiful, shiny red apple out to Snow White. "Go on, have a bite."

The animals sensed something terrible was about to happen and emerged from their hiding places. They went outside and tried to chase the hag away. Snow White didn't understand why they were behaving badly, so she shooed them off. As she invited the old woman inside, the animals raced into the forest to get help from the dwarfs.

The animals ran and flew as quickly as they could. When they finally reached the diamond mine, they found the dwarfs hard at work. The animals pulled and tugged at their clothing, trying to tell them that Snow White was in danger.

"They aren't actin' this way for nothin'," Grumpy said.

"Maybe the queen's got Snow White," Sleepy said with a yawn.

The queen! That was it! There was no time to lose. The dwarfs grabbed their picks and clubs and ran to the rescue.

They didn't know it, but they were too late. Snow White had already taken a bite of the poisoned apple and was lying lifeless on the floor.

The queen cackled with glee. "The only thing that can save her now is a kiss from the one who truly loves her, but no prince will ever find her in this great big forest!"

Still in her disguise, the wicked queen ran out of the cottage. The bright sunshine had been replaced by dark, threatening clouds, and the air was damp and cold.

At that moment, the dwarfs neared the clearing and saw the queen fleeing into the forest. With the help of the animals, they chased her through the trees. The sound of thunder boomed overhead and lightning flashed in the sky.

The rain began to
pour down. The dwarfs
could hardly see, but they
managed to trap the queen
on a narrow cliff. She began
prying a large boulder
loose, intending to send it
toppling onto the dwarfs
below. The queen's laughter
echoed as the boulder
began to move.

"Look out!" cried Grumpy
to the others.

Suddenly, a bolt of lightning split the air and struck the part of the cliff where the queen was standing. The piece of rock broke away and sent the queen falling into the blackness far below, never to be heard from again.

When the weary dwarfs returned to the cottage, they found the poisoned Snow White. Unable to awaken her, they laid her across their beds. Tears streamed down their faces as they knelt beside her motionless body.

Even in death, Snow
White was so beautiful that
the dwarfs could not bring
themselves to bury her.
Instead they laid her in a
casket of glass and gold,
and they kept watch over
her day and night.

Far away in another part of the kingdom, the handsome young prince heard of a beautiful maiden who slept in the forest. Hoping that this was the princess he had fallen in love with at the well, he searched far and wide to find her. One day when he was out riding, he came upon her casket. Gently lifting the glass lid, he gazed on Snow White's beauty once more.

The prince bent down and softly placed a kiss on Snow White's lips. Then he knelt and bowed his head in silence, surrounded by the animals and the seven dwarfs.

At the moment, the princess began to stir. She
sat up and rubbed her eyes.

Snow White was alive!

Joyously, the prince gathered her in his arms, while
shouts of jubilation rang out around them. The dwarfs
hugged each other with happiness.

Snow White kissed each dwarf good-bye. Then the prince lifted
her up onto his horse and led her to his castle on the hill. Though the
dwarfs would miss Snow White, their hearts were glad, because they
knew that she and her prince would live happily ever after.

Published by Penguin Books USA Inc., 375 Hudson Street, New York, New York 10014
©1993 The Walt Disney Company. All rights reserved. No part of this publication may be reproduced, stored in a
retrieval system, or transmitted in any form, by any means, electronic, mechanical, photocopying or otherwise,
without first obtaining written permission of the copyright owners.
Mouse Works is a registered trademark of The Walt Disney Company.
Printed in the United States of America.

ISBN 0-453-03166-8

1 0 9 8 7 6 5 4 3 2